Written and illustrated by
Adam Hargreaves

Little Miss Dotty had been to the shops. And she had bought something. Which is all quite normal, but what she had bought was far from normal.

She had bought a submarine! And why had she bought a submarine?

Well, that was the question Mr Happy asked when he went round for tea.

"I don't know," admitted Little Miss Dotty, with a shrug of her shoulders.

She lives in the middle of a wood, in the middle of the countryside, in the middle of Nonsenseland, where the grass is blue and the leaves are pink.

It is a very long way from the sea.

And she had bought a submarine!

Dotty by name and dotty by nature.

"We will have to take your submarine to Seatown,"
said Mr Happy.

And so they did.

In Seatown they met Little Miss Sunshine.

She was very excited at the sight of the submarine.

"That's just what I need," she said. "I am organising an underwater expedition to find the lost city of Atlantis."

"I'm always losing things," said Little Miss Dotty. "But I have never lost a city. We will help you find it!"

They put together a crew and went to sea.

"Help! We're sinking!" cried Little Miss Dotty, as the submarine dived under the waves.

Mr Happy explained how a submarine works.

"So," said Little Miss Dotty, "which way to Atlantis?"

"It's a lost city," said Little Miss Sunshine.

"And …" said Little Miss Dotty.

"Well, it wouldn't be lost if I knew where it was," explained Little Miss Sunshine.

"Maybe we will find a mermaid," said Little Miss Dotty.

"Don't be silly," laughed Little Miss Sunshine, "mermaids aren't real!"

On their search to find Atlantis they went swimming in a reef. All the brightly-coloured coral was very beautiful.

"It's so pretty. It's like an underwater garden," said Little Miss Fickle. "Or maybe a shop full of sweets? Or maybe a colourful painting?"

Little Miss Fickle can never make up her mind.

In amongst the coral were lots of different fish.
There were big fish like Mr Greedy.

There were small fish like Little Miss Tiny.

There were grumpy-looking
fish like Mr Grumpy.

There were jellyfish like Mr Jelly.

There were skinny fish like Mr Skinny.

And there were spotty fish that Little Miss Dotty liked very much.

What a lot of fish there were in the sea!

"That's an electric eel," pointed out Mr Happy.
"Don't touch it!" he cried.

But it was too late.

Poor Mr Greedy had been zapped.

"Now I know what a fried fish feels like," said Mr Greedy,
shakily, once they had brought him safely back onboard
the submarine.

Their search for Atlantis took them to the bottom of the ocean. The deeper the submarine dived, the darker it became, until it was pitch black on the ocean floor. But even this deep down there were fish to find.

Very strange looking fish!

"They look like aliens from outer space," said Mr Happy.

The fish even had their own lights.

They glowed in the dark.

There was no sign of Atlantis in the depths of the ocean, so the submarine began to rise. Suddenly, a whale loomed up out of the murky water.

A sleepy whale.

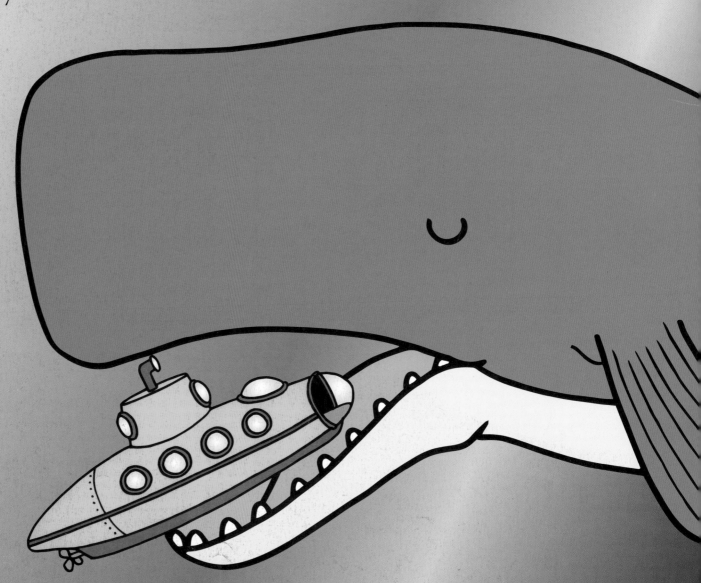

There was no sign of Atlantis in the depths of the ocean, so the submarine began to rise. Suddenly, a whale loomed up out of the murky water.

A sleepy whale.

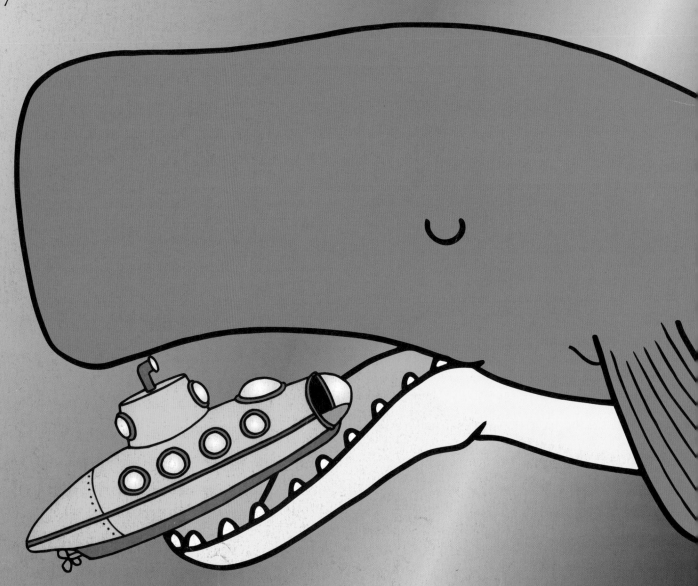

The whale opened its mouth and yawned an enormous yawn.

And swallowed the submarine!

In one enormous gulp.

"Oh help," squeaked Mr Jelly.

They were inside the whale.

"Oh help!" shrieked Mr Jelly, much louder this time. "We've been swallowed by a whale! Oh my! Oh gosh! We'll never get out! It's a calamity! How will we ever escape?"

But nobody in the submarine had an answer.

Submarines are not something that whales normally eat and it quite disagreed with this particular whale.

The whale's stomach rumbled. An even bigger rumble than an empty Mr Greedy tummy.

The submarine had given the whale indigestion.

The whale burped. An almighty great burp. A burp that echoed around the ocean.

BURP!

And, as if it had been fired from a cannon, the submarine shot right back out of the whale's mouth.

Which was very lucky. But that was not all, because the whale had helped them in their search.

The submarine now lay in the ruins of an ancient city. An ancient city that had been submerged beneath the sea.

"That's Atlantis!" cried Little Miss Dotty.

"How on earth could you know that?" asked Little Miss Sunshine.

"Look, there's a sign," said Little Miss Dotty pointing to a stone signpost.

And carved in the stone was the word 'Atlantis'.

"Oh," said Little Miss Sunshine.

They found all sorts of things amongst the ruins.

Little Miss Sunshine was very excited.

There were statues, vases, coins, a sword and even an ancient ship.

It was a whole lost civilization.

But Little Miss Tiny made
the greatest discovery.

She had found a mermaid!

"How extraordinary!" exclaimed Little Miss Sunshine, when Little Miss Tiny showed her.

"Well I never!" cried Mr Happy.

"I can't believe my eyes!" declared Mr Greedy.

"I told you we might see a mermaid," said Little Miss Dotty.

And she had been right.

Which is something that does not happen very often to Little Miss Dotty.